Annie and Snowball and the Wedding Day

The Thirteenth Book of Their Adventures

Cynthia Rylant

Illustrated by Suçie Stevenson

READY-TO-READ

SIMON SPOTLIGHT

New York   London   Toronto   Sydney   New Delhi

To Everlasting Love— S. S.

SIMON SPOTLIGHT

An imprint of Simon & Schuster Children's Publishing Division
1230 Avenue of the Americas, New York, New York 10020
Text copyright © 2014 by Cynthia Rylant
Illustrations copyright © 2014 by Suçie Stevenson
SIMON SPOTLIGHT, READY-TO-READ, and colophon are
registered trademarks of Simon & Schuster, Inc.
For information about special discounts for bulk purchases, please contact
Simon & Schuster Special Sales at 1-866-506-1949 or business@simonandschuster.com.
The Simon & Schuster Speakers Bureau can bring authors to your live event. For more
information or to book an event contact the Simon & Schuster Speakers Bureau at
1-866-248-3049 or visit our website at www.simonspeakers.com.
Designed by Tom Daly
The text of this book was set in Goudy Old Style.
The illustrations for this book were rendered in pen-and-ink and watercolor.
Manufactured in China 1013 SCP
First Simon Spotlight edition 2014
2 4 6 8 10 9 7 5 3 1
Library of Congress Cataloging-in-Publication Data
Rylant, Cynthia.
Annie and Snowball and the wedding day : the thirteenth book of their adventures /
by Cynthia Rylant ; illustrated by Suçie Stevenson. — First edition.
pages cm. — (Annie and Snowball ; 13) (Ready-to-read)
Summary: "Annie loves living with her dad and her bunny, Snowball.
But she wants her dad to find someone to love. Then he meets a woman
named Martha. Soon it is time for a wedding!"— Provided by publisher.
[1. Remarriage—Fiction. 2. Fathers and daughters—Fiction. 3. Stepmothers—Fiction.
4. Rabbits—Fiction.] I. Title.
PZ7.R982Anv 2014
[E]—dc23
2013030031
ISBN 978-1-4169-7485-7
ISBN 978-1-4169-8249-4 (eBook)

Contents

The Right Someone   5

Singing   11

Tea and Sugar Buns   17

Yes!   25

Everlasting   35

The Right Someone

Annie and her father and her bunny,
Snowball, lived next door
to her cousin Henry
and his big dog, Mudge.
It was fun living next door
to Henry's family.

5

Henry's dad and Annie's dad built
things together.

Henry and Annie explored things together.

And Snowball and Mudge chewed
things together.

It was fun being families side by side.

Yet something was missing.
What was missing was someone for
Annie's dad to love.
He was a good dad.
And he would be a good husband if the
right someone came along.

One day that someone showed up.

Singing

It was in May when the birds were
singing that Annie's dad
started singing too.

He sang while he cooked.

He sang while he cleaned.

He looked so happy.

"I have met a very nice person,"
Annie's dad told her one day.

"Her name is Martha," he said.
"She loves children and bunnies,
and she has a cat."

"What is her cat's name?" asked Annie.

"Rose Cat," said her dad.

Annie smiled.

Rose Cat and Martha.

Life was about to change.

Tea and Sugar Buns

Soon Annie went to meet
Rose Cat and Martha.
Annie was a little nervous.
What if Martha did not like her?

17

But as soon as Annie stepped
into Martha's home, Annie knew
everything would be all right.
Martha was soft-spoken and kind.

Rose Cat sat on Annie's lap and purred
while they all had tea and sugar buns.

When it was time for Annie to go home, Martha loaned her one of Martha's favorite books.
It was about a girl and a lost pony.

On her way home Annie sang.

Yes!

Things changed so wonderfully.
Martha visited Annie's house often.

25

She became good friends with Henry's
mother.

Rose Cat became good friends with
Snowball and Mudge.

Martha was always happy and kind.
And Annie missed her when she left.
So did Annie's dad.

They needed Martha with them
all the time.

The day finally came when Annie's dad
asked Martha to marry him.
Martha said, "Yes!"

And soon wedding plans were being
made for a spring wedding.
Plans and plans and plans!

Annie tried on twenty different dresses
until she found the loveliest one.

It had an organdy petticoat and a velvet
sash.

Annie couldn't wait for the wedding day!

Everlasting

On a warm April day everyone
Annie loved
gathered in a little church garden.
The wedding was so beautiful
that it made Annie cry.

After the wedding everyone went to
Henry's house for cupcakes.

The cupcakes were decorated
with sparkles and roses.

37

There were fancy carrot sticks for bunnies,

and fancy tuna puffs for cats,

and fancy crackers for big drooly dogs.

Annie could not remember ever having
such a day.
Hope and happiness was all around her.
No longer was anything missing.
And love felt everlasting.